D1442478

ISBN 0-8249-5859-4

First published in this format in 2003 by Ideals Children's Books
An imprint of Ideals Publications, a division of Guideposts
535 Metroplex Drive, Suite 250, Nashville, Tennessee 37211
www.idealsbooks.com

Previously published by Lang Books, Delafield, Wisconsin

Library of Congress CIP data on file

Printed and bound in Italy

10 9 8 7 6 5 4 3 2 1

The Visit

WRITTEN BY

Mark Kimball Moulton

ILLUSTRATED BY

Susan Winget

ideals children's books™

Nashville, Tennessee

Since *The Night Before Christmas* first appeared,
we're certain many have wondered about the story
behind the story. How did this cherished poem
come to be? What inspired a principled,
highly educated biblical scholar to create such
a tender and magical Christmas tale?

The answer, according to Moore family legend, is simple—
it was the heartfelt love of a parent for his child.

We are honored to share this story in the same spirit in which
Clement C. Moore first offered *The Night Before Christmas* many years
ago . . . as a gift of love to all little children everywhere, forevermore.

Dinghy, Susan, and Mark

Happy Christmas

Presented to

_____

From

_____

On this date

_____

Dear Readers and Lovers of Christmas,
I would like to share with you my wonderful Christmas memory.

In 1822, my grandfather's grandfather, Clement Clarke Moore,
created a delightful Christmas poem for his ailing daughter as his
Christmas gift to her that year. He did not realize at the time
that it was destined to become a classic.

His gift was first known as *An Account of a Visit from St. Nicholas*
but is now better known as *The Night Before Christmas*.
The following account is true as I know it and has been lovingly
passed down from generation to generation in my family.
I do hope you enjoy the story as much as I enjoy telling it.

With Christmas love and joy,

Dinghy Sharp

Part One

"To Grandfather's House We Go"
Michigan to New York
Late December, 1936

It was late in December,
and I, but a child,
when our dear mother bent down
and hugged us and smiled.

"Come. Let's pack our valises,"
she said to us all,
"for a visit with Granddad,"
she said, I recall.

Well, this news made us all
feel a little bit giddy,
for we'd never seen
Granddad's home in the city!

So we packed what we needed
and traveled by train—
our delight was apparent
and hard to contain!

Oh, the train ride was lovely,
and I'll never forget
all the sights and the sounds
and the folks that we met.

The next morning we woke, and to our great surprise,
there stood New York City, right before our own eyes!

People hustled and bustled and ran everywhere.
It was noisy and hectic and so thrilling there!

The buildings rose higher than any I'd seen.
I tried counting floors but gave up at nineteen!

Mother hailed a big taxi, which to us was a thrill,
and we climbed in the back seat and sat very still.

We peered out the windows, our eyes open wide,
as the city flew by us on that first taxi ride.

All the stores were a-twinkle, with clothing and toys,
and we felt very glad we'd been good girls and boys!

Before long, we arrived
at our grandfather's place—
a great building so lofty,
it soared up in space!

We walked through the lobby
and up to a door—
it opened, we entered,
and it rose from the floor!

Another new thrill,
this small room that could fly,
safely taking us to Granddad's
home in the sky!

We knocked on his door,
and he welcomed us in;
then he gathered us to him
and exclaimed with a grin:

"I've a gift that I've wanted
to share with you all.
Something my granddad gave me
when I was quite small."

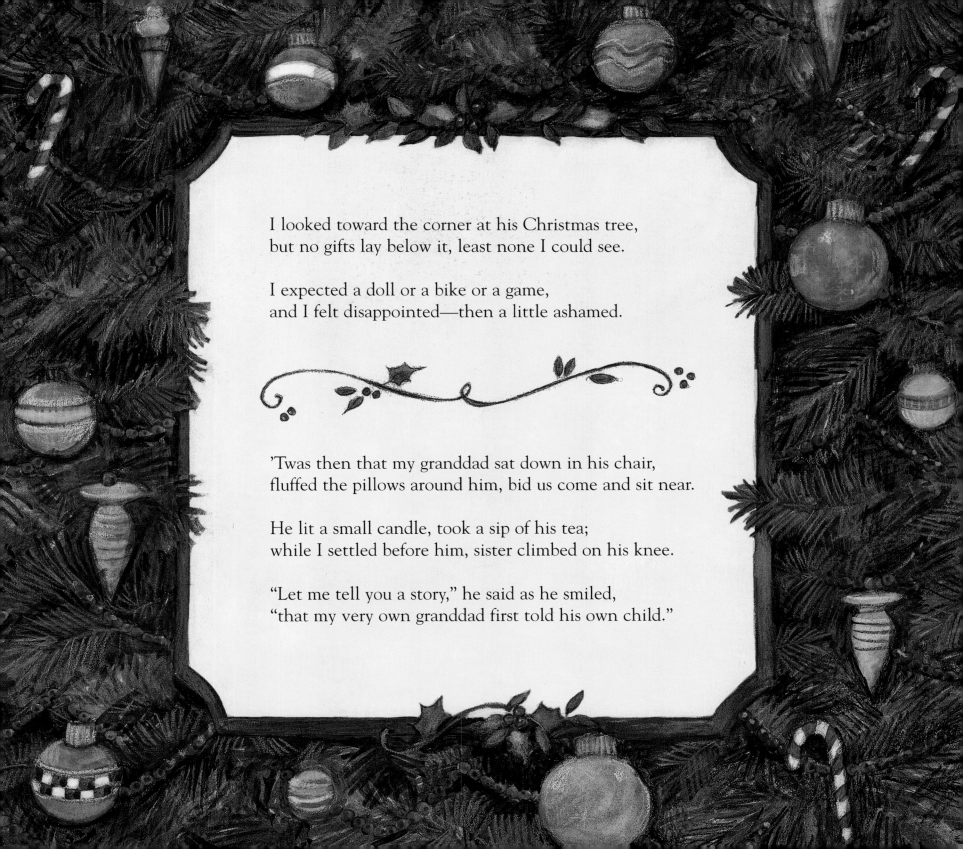

I looked toward the corner at his Christmas tree,
but no gifts lay below it, least none I could see.

I expected a doll or a bike or a game,
and I felt disappointed—then a little ashamed.

'Twas then that my granddad sat down in his chair,
fluffed the pillows around him, bid us come and sit near.

He lit a small candle, took a sip of his tea;
while I settled before him, sister climbed on his knee.

"Let me tell you a story," he said as he smiled,
"that my very own granddad first told his own child."

Part Two

"Granddad's Account"
New York City
Late December, 1936

"I shall start out this tale
with some little-known facts
that have long been forgotten
or slipped through the cracks.

"Dr. Clement Clarke Moore
was my grandfather's name,
but to all he was 'Papa,'
friends and family the same.

"Papa Moore was a scholar—
he wrote many fine texts,
though none are more famous
than the one I'll tell next.

"He conceived his new poem
in eighteen-twenty-two,
on Christmas Eve day.
Yes, the legend is true.

"So much has been changed
since he wrote his good verse,
some things for the better
and some for the worse.

"Take clothing, for instance—
though this might seem shocking—
as children, each night
we would wash out our stockings!

"We'd rub them and scrub them
and hang them to dry,
'by the chimney with care'
as this tale will imply!

"Now some good folks today
might just readily assume
that we'd hang up those stockings
to dry in our rooms.

"And though I admit
that it would have been nice,
I'm afraid if we had,
they'd have frozen to ice.

"For the bedrooms back then
were so rarely with heat
that it often took hours
just to warm up our feet!

"And this explains why,
when we took a long nap,
Mama Moore wore her kerchief
and Papa, a bed cap!"

Granddad gave us a nod,
cleared his throat, sipped his tea,
then resumed his account
of how things used to be.

"'Sugarplum' is a word
that's unheard-of nowadays,
but we made them with fruit
rolled in sugary glaze.

"Then we'd wrap them and store them
and soon they'd become
the delicious, jeweled candy
we called 'sugarplum.'

"They glittered by firelight
and tasted supreme,
and often that vision
would dance in my dreams!

"Papa's farm," he continued, "sat on an old street,
in a section called Chelsea that was somewhat elite.

"His house, tall and handsome, had windows galore,
which caused quite a problem he could not ignore.

"For in winter, the wind blew through each window crack;
not having storm windows was quite a drawback.

"So dear Papa hung shutters both inside and out,
which explains how this line of his poem came about:

"'Away to the window I flew like a flash,
Tore open the shutters and threw up the sash.'

"One last line of the poem
that I'd like to explain
is 'More rapid than eagles
his coursers they came.'

"As you know, in the winter
in Papa Moore's day,
many folks often traveled
through snow in a sleigh.

"And teams that pulled sleighs,
whether horses or deer,
were commonly known as
'coursers' in that year!"

Part Three

"A Visit to Papa's"
Chelsea, New York
Christmas Eve, 1822

Then Granddad became quiet,
settled back in his chair,
took a sip of his tea,
ran a hand through his hair.

He murmured so softly,
"Now, how did it go?
I must tell you exactly . . .
must recount it just so.

"Ahhh, yes. I remember,"
he said soft and low.
"It was Christmas Eve day . . ."
he began, soft and slow.

"Twilight was just falling upon the Moore house, when out of the kitchen came Papa Moore's spouse.

"'Papa dear,' she inquired,
'will you travel to town
and buy a goose from the butcher
'fore he closes down?

"'And don't forget that you promised
your daughter upstairs
a new story for Christmas
to lighten her cares.'

"You see, their daughter was sickly,
quite feeble and lame,
confined to her bed.
Charity Moore was her name.

"And the one gift that Charity
had asked for that year
was a simple, new story
from her Papa dear.

"So Papa rushed to the barn,
harnessed coursers to sleigh,
and with a flick of the reins,
they were soon on their way.

"The night sky was clear,
filled with twinkling stars,
but that was to change
before they'd traveled too far.

"For dark, stormy clouds
soon began to roll in
and to fill the night sky
where the stars had once been.

"And before my dear Papa
could whisper, 'Jack Frost,'
a thick snow was falling
and he soon became lost.

"But his coursers, those horses, had traveled each day
to the town, so they knew where to pull his good sleigh.

"They crossed through the meadow, through the forest and stream,
as if they were floating through a mid-winter's dream.

"But just as they reached the far edge of the river,
the horses pulled up. They stomped and they quivered,

"and blew steam from their noses, and they huffed and they puffed,
as if saying to Papa, 'We've gone far enough!'

"And suddenly, just like magic, the snow disappeared,
and the moon shone its face as the clouds slowly cleared.
And the wind started blowing, which made everything freeze,
and the snow turned to diamonds on the fields and the trees.

"And the moon on the breast of the new-fallen snow
gave a luster of midday to objects below.

"Papa Moore was enchanted,
mesmerized by the scene;
'twas the most beautiful sight
that he'd ever seen!

"He looked down the hill,
toward the village below,
watching friends running last-minute
chores through the snow.

"And from his lofty perch,
in his sleigh on the hill,
Papa caught a slight movement
behind the old mill.

"He watched as a figure
in red coat and hood,
drew a sled through the town,
full of fresh-chopped firewood.

"He recognized the old woodman
as the kindly Jan-Peter,
who was well loved in town,
for no man could be sweeter.

"He had a white beard
and a heart made of gold.
He was rotund and jolly
and appeared very old.

"He smoked a clay pipe
as he managed his chores,
his nose, cherry red
from his work out-of-doors.

"Now Jan-Peter was known
as a teller of tales,
who enchanted his friends
with his charming portrayals.

"He'd sit by the stove
at the general store,
encircled by children
curled up on the floor.

"And he'd entertain them
with his tales of delight,
of the Dutchman, Saint Nicholas,
and his journeys at night.

"And if they were good,
he would give each a treat—
a delicious, sweet sugarplum
candy to eat!

"But this night, he appeared
to be up to no good
as he traveled through town
with his wagon of wood.

"He'd creep down an alley,
then reach back in his sleigh,
leave a small pile of *something*,
then he'd hurry away.

"And as Papa sat watching,
it soon became clear,
what Jan-Peter was doing
in the alleyways there.

"He was leaving his tinder
beside every door
of the folks in the town
who were hungry and poor.

"Jan-Peter was giving
the one gift that he could—
a warm Christmas for all
with the gift of his wood.

"Papa's eyes filled with tears as he watched his old friend,
who hadn't a penny nor a dollar to spend,
offer kindness and love to those people in need;
and he thought, 'What a good man. What a true saint, indeed!'

"And as Papa sat there, so content in his sleigh,
on that hill, Christmas Eve, on that long-ago day,

"he thought of his daughter and her simple request,
and he thought of his family and how they were blessed.

"And he thought of Jan-Peter and his selfless, good deeds,
and he thought of how love is all the world needs.

"And 'twas then, in that instant, Papa knew he would write
a new Christmas story for his daughter that night.

"He would fill it with magic,
with such wonder and joy
that it'd be known the world over
by all girls and boys.

"It's become a great classic
that I'm sure you've heard of—
this gift to his daughter . . .
Papa's gift of his love.

"Oh, and yes,
Papa did make the butcher in time
and brought Mamma her goose
while conceiving his rhyme.

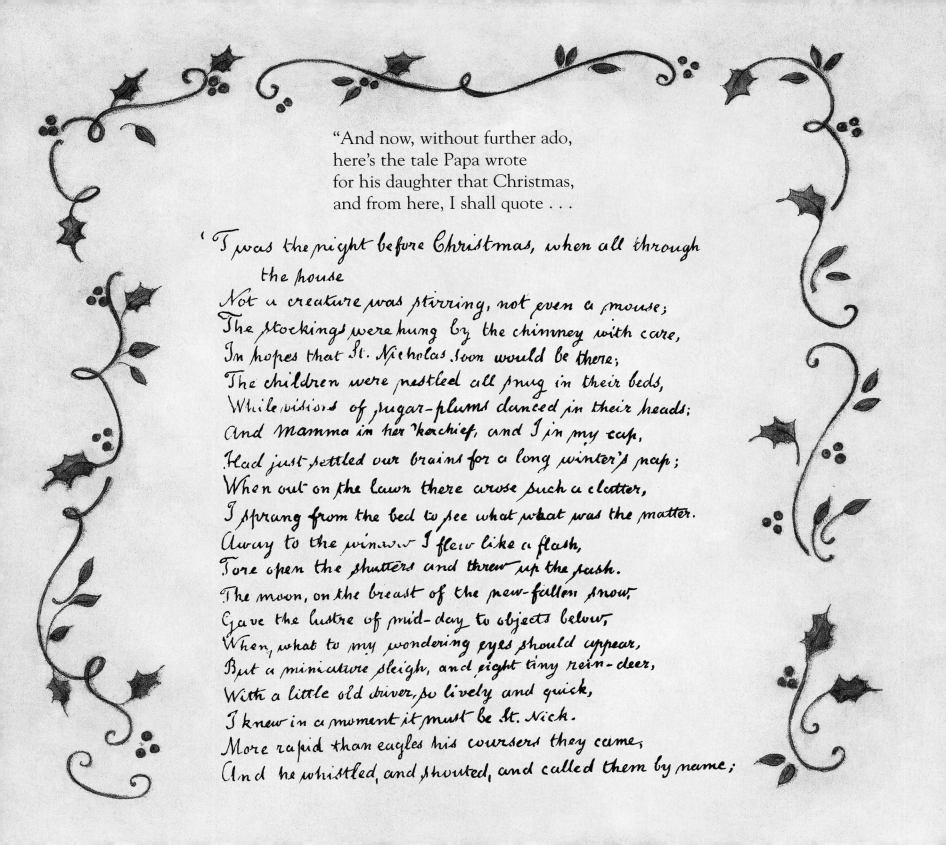

"And now, without further ado,
here's the tale Papa wrote
for his daughter that Christmas,
and from here, I shall quote . . .

'Twas the night before Christmas, when all through
        the house
Not a creature was stirring, not even a mouse;
The stockings were hung by the chimney with care,
In hopes that St. Nicholas soon would be there;
The children were nestled all snug in their beds,
While visions of sugar-plums danced in their heads;
And Mamma in her 'kerchief, and I in my cap,
Had just settled our brains for a long winter's nap;
When out on the lawn there arose such a clatter,
I sprang from the bed to see what what was the matter.
Away to the window I flew like a flash,
Tore open the shutters and threw up the sash.
The moon, on the breast of the new-fallen snow,
Gave the lustre of mid-day to objects below,
When, what to my wondering eyes should appear,
But a miniature sleigh, and eight tiny rein-deer,
With a little old driver, so lively and quick,
I knew in a moment it must be St. Nick.
More rapid than eagles his coursers they came,
And he whistled, and shouted, and called them by name;

"Now, Dasher! now, Dancer! now, Prancer and Vixen!
On, Comet! on, Cupid! on, Donder and Blitzen!
To the top of the porch! to the top of the wall!
Now dash away! dash away! dash away all!"

As dry leaves that before the wild hurricane fly,

When they meet with an obstacle, mount to the sky;

So up to the house-top the coursers they flew,

With the sleigh full of Toys, and St. Nicholas too.

And then, in a twinkling, I heard on the roof

The prancing and pawing of each little hoof —

As I drew in my head, and was turning around,

Down the chimney St. Nicholas came with a bound.

He was dressed all in fur, from his head to his foot,

And his clothes were all tarnished with ashes and soot;

A bundle of Toys he had flung on his back,

And he look'd like a pedlar just opening his pack.

His eyes — how they twinkled! his dimples how merry!

His cheeks were like roses, his nose like a cherry!

His droll little mouth was drawn up like a bow

And the beard of his chin was as white as the snow;

The stump of a pipe he held tight in his teeth,

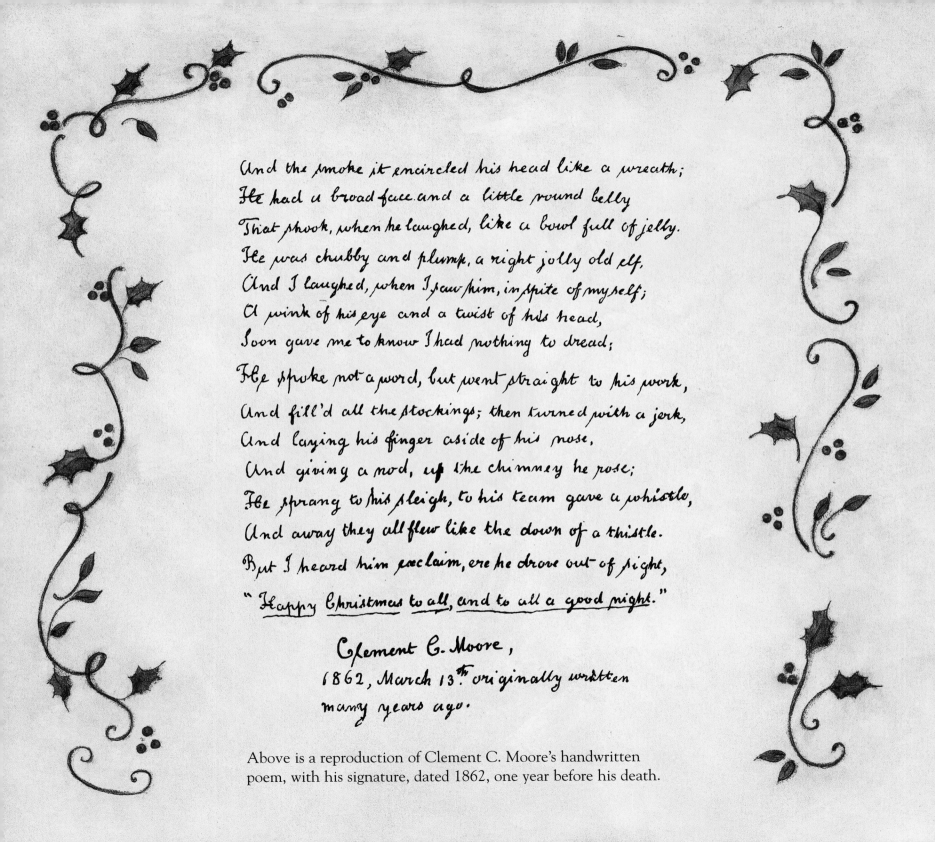

And the smoke it encircled his head like a wreath;
He had a broad face and a little round belly
That shook, when he laughed, like a bowl full of jelly.
He was chubby and plump, a right jolly old elf,
And I laughed, when I saw him, in spite of myself;
A wink of his eye and a twist of his head,
Soon gave me to know I had nothing to dread;

He spoke not a word, but went straight to his work,
And fill'd all the stockings; then turned with a jerk,
And laying his finger aside of his nose,
And giving a nod, up the chimney he rose;
He sprang to his sleigh, to his team gave a whistle,
And away they all flew like the down of a thistle.
But I heard him exclaim, ere he drove out of sight,
"Happy Christmas to all, and to all a good night."

Clement C. Moore,
1862, March 13th originally written
many years ago.

Above is a reproduction of Clement C. Moore's handwritten
poem, with his signature, dated 1862, one year before his death.